CLICHÉ AND WIND
GO HITCHHIKING

MARCEL ST. PIERRE

CLICHÉ
— AND —
WIND
GO
HITCHHIKING

MKZ
PRESS

Issued in print and electronic formats

ISBN 978-0-9949409-4-0 (bound)
ISBN 978-0-9949409-5-7 (Kindle)

Cover design: Mike Butler
Photos by: Ali Eisner

MKZ Press
1621 Pilgrims Way
Oakville, Ontario, Canada L6M 2H2
mkzpress@mkz.com

Table of Contents

Foreword

These are busy, busy times.

Ask any friend or acquaintance you run into and they'll be telling you how occupied they are before the words "How ya doing?" have left your lips. Listening to their tales of exhaustion, you'll be surprised that they can squeeze in a blink and a breath between saving the world and succeeding at life.

Life may not be as bustling as we present it, but perception is usually reality, so we desperately need small and fun things to distract us from our big and boring (and hectic) lives.

Just in time, Marcel has created those distractions.

These stories are perfect because our diversions from reality need to be short and weird. If they're long and weird, the departure isn't temporary enough and we balk at the commitment. If they're short and normal, they're just mundane vignettes of an adult life lived out on Instagram. No, we need short, and we need weird. And we need them printed and bound together in user-friendly book form. Done, done, and done.

Sure, you have stuff to do (we all have stuff to do) but hey, Jeepers Magoo, ignore your beating heart and pull over. Don't pass out. Don't hyperventilate. Don't go into shock. These stories are like getting naked and running through a field of your dreams. They're like finding an actual radio station playing Miles Davis while you wonder if you turned the stove off.

Throughout *cliché and wind go hitchhiking*, I wasn't just rewarded by the exit from the everyday, I was inspired by the craft. It's one thing to think of an abstract idea or unique premise. It's quite another to stitch it together with writing that delivers on the promise.

Let's face it, we're all hungry and exhausted and trying to make the best of it. Wonderful distractions like this collection help us get there with a smile on our face. Thanks, Marcel.

Ron Tite
Co-Author Everyone's an Artist (or at least they should be)
Founder & CEO, Church & State

Moreword

I first met Marcel St. Pierre in 2003, when we were both working on a CBC children's television show.

We knew instantly, eyeing each other, that neither of us belonged there.

Years later, I was flattered when Marcel asked me to perform at a show he co-hosted called *Other People's Stuff*. The premise of the show was that you had to perform someone else's material. I painstakingly reconstructed a Sandra Bernhard monologue and some Chris Rock stand-up. I appreciated that Marcel tested me. Of course, the show, like much of Marcel's work on stage as an improvisor and sketch comedian, was terrific. Despite his mild-mannered appearance, here was someone always ready to surprise.

Now, he has written a book of short stories, most of them quite funny and all of them rather

11

inventive. As a writer, he embraces worlds, personifies animals, inhabits secret places, and explores hidden realms, all of which is to say that they are really well written. This stuff is delightful. It's hard to pick a fave, but *cliché and wind go hitchhiking* is on par with the best of David Sedaris.

So once again, Marcel St. Pierre has surprised me.

He's not just a good comedian, he's also a great storyteller. And, get this, I just found out that this is his *second* book.

Can't wait for the third.

Paul Bellini
Co-Author, Buddy Babylon: The Buddy Cole Story
Writer and Towel Guy, The Kids in the Hall

Otherwords

... quirky, zany and funny... I encourage you, dive right in!

Ali Hassan
Comedian, Chef, Host of CBC Radio's Canada Reads

... brisk storytelling. compelling characters... stories that tweak and baffle... nutty shit that slaps you across the face like a flying carp... I laughed out loud. I did not roll on the floor laughing, but only because I have very comfortable, sturdy furniture...

Dan Redican
Comedian, Writer, Producer, Director,
Frantics co-founder and former Henson puppeteer

.... a fabulous collision of reality, humour and doubt... an observation of the absurd manifestations of life...

Lucie Pagé
Screenwriter, copywriter, story editor

Twistedly unexpected, delightfully bonkers and highly recommended. When a book makes you laugh so much that your husband comes downstairs to your office to find out what the hell is going on you know it's a winner.

Marilla Wex
Actor, Writer, Comedian
The Beaverton Foreign Correspondent

... an utterly fun escape from the real world, with the added bonus of making you laugh... ... so many weird and wonderful worlds with equally captivating characters...

Maryam Siddiqi
Editor, writer, photographer
Globe & Mail, National Post, Reader's Digest

... wild, wacky, and wonderful... cleverly conceived and artfully crafted...

Gina Sorell
Author, Mothers and Other Strangers

"These writings are flat-out lies," I bellowed to my wife, who was in another city at the time. It was then brought to my attention this book falls into a specific literary genre known as 'fiction,' meaning the events portrayed within its pages are entirely made up and in no way occurred. Only then was I able to appreciate the high quality and comedic heft of *cliché and wind go hitchhiking* ... a worthy companion to such beloved non-nonfiction anthologies as Steve Martin's *Cruel Shoes*, Jon Stewart's *Naked Pictures Of Famous People*, and some third example of a well-received book.

Steven Shehori
Writer, AV Club, Splitsider, Huffington Post

... with the conviction of a man using word dice... the author combines the innocent language of *The Hardy Boys* and *Dr. Seuss* with the gentle comedy of H.P. Lovecraft... Have you ever read a book you didn't understand until the very end only to realize "My God, he has written about a universal experience that ties me to all humanity because we have all lived it!" This is not that book.

Albert Howell
Writer, Late Night With Jimmy Fallon

... off-beat wit, breezy writing style and obviously madcap imagination... more storyline twists and turns than the Ikea store showroom, and more oddball characters than the 2am last call subway train...

Jory Nash,
Award-winning singer/songwriter/producer

... delightful... nonsensical... Well, I'm not wrong, am I? Sorry I snapped there, just annoyed because now I have to go try and write a funny book, too. There's one French word by my count, but you can skip it.

Jeremy Woodcock,
Writer, Toronto Life, This Hour Has 22 Minutes

Dedication

To Gerald Arthur
Roommate,
musician,
merry mischief-maker,
provider of kibbeh,
friend and
hero.

You are remembered and loved.
Rest in peace, buddy.
We miss you.

Kiosk

Gram had never noticed this kiosk before. It was stark white, with a tiny white placard bearing the word 'kiosk' in black lettering. Curious, he came to a stop several feet away from it and looked around.

There was no salesperson to be seen, no products on display, no photos or pamphlets or any other information to give him a clue as to what 'kiosk' might be or what it sold.

He took a final step up to the counter.

"Nghah!" snorted Gram, startled to see an exactly two-inches-shorter than counter height woman sitting on a short stool directly behind the kiosk.

"Frghsh!" exclaimed the exactly two-inches-shorter than counter height woman who had also been startled at Gram's sudden, looming appearance.

She wore a white lab coat, and had a jet-black, straight bowl haircut that may or may not have been a wig. She wore no makeup save for starkly penciled-in eyebrows at least three centimeters higher above her greenish eyes than would be considered reasonable, giving her a perpetually surprised countenance. Her left incisor protruded two inches over her closed mouth, such that it resembled a small tusk.

They stared at each other a moment.

"Uh..." began Gram. "I just sort of noticed the sign here and wondered–"

"We sell dreams," she interrupted impatiently, walking out to him from behind the counter. "First one's free. Here." And before he could protest, she grabbed his hand.

Instantly, he was transported to a multicolored field of wildflowers, and he was filled with peace, and love, and... joy? He giggled, then he began laughing. He was filled with such childlike wonder that he began to run through the flowers.

He was alive! He was running! He was jumping! He was laughing! He was happy! He was naked! And then he realized he was frolicking hand in hand with someone..?

Who was it?

His new best friend?

His lover?

He looked over in mid-jump.

He saw the woman from the kiosk, also naked, her mid-jump breasts pointing wildly in counter-intuitive directions. Her gaze met his, and she made a monstrous, horrible sound which might have been meant to be a pleasant laugh.

As Gram's face contorted into a silent scream, her lips puckered like a tired sphincter and she moved in for a tusky, unsmiling, tongue-first kiss...

"GAH!" said Gram, coming out of the dream, pulling his hand back with a gasp.

"How many you want?" she asked, walking back behind the counter to complete the transaction.

Gram ran away quickly, and 'Tusky' – as he would call her when retelling the story – had lost another sale. She sat down dejectedly on her short stool. She knew her brand was an acquired taste, but she hoped it would catch on soon; downtown mall kiosk rentals were expensive.

Modern Venice

A couple approached a mooring near the Rialto Bridge to enquire about hiring a gondolier for a romantic ride along the Venetian canals.

"Si, very romantic, very good guide, very good price," said Enzo, a kindly, middle-aged man wearing the traditional black pants, striped shirt and hat of his trade. "Please, only to step on my gondola and Enzo take very good care of you."

"Mi scusi, per favore," called another gondolier, a younger man, who was just tying up his gondola a few posts over. "You would safely more to come with me."

"Eh! Antonio, zitto! They come with me," snapped Enzo. "Vaffanculo!" The couple shifted uncomfortably at the sudden and harsh downturn in vibe. Enzo smiled at them broadly and extended his hand invitingly towards his gondola. "Please, come!"

The couple acquiesced and moved closer to boarding the boat, but Antonio piped up again. "Eh! Eh! Eh! Mister, miss, non tocare, eh? Don't touch him! Lui è un cannibale!"

"Eh! Antonio! Zitto! Shut uppa you face, eh?!" menaced Enzo, flicking his thumb against his top front teeth at the younger man. "Come, he is not right in the head, forgive him," he said again smilingly to the couple, "This way."

"Wait," said the woman, consulting her Google translate app. "Did he just call you a cannibal?" She called over to Antonio. "Did you call him a cannibal?"

"Si, si! Enzo è un cannibale, un cannibale – vedere! Look! See!" replied Antonio, holding up a bandaged stump for a hand.

The couple took a startled step back.

Annoyed, Enzo picked up a tibia lying at the bottom of his boat and threw it, hitting young Antonio in the temple and sending him overboard.

The couple, now terrified, ran away.

"You so lucky the gondolier polizia already give me two strikes!" yelled Enzo, shaking his fist at Antonio as he came up for air.

The Courting of Constance Croonstopper

It was early in the evening, and Jeepers Magoo sat on his front porch swing.

He was waiting for something to happen.

Sometimes he'd sit like this for days.

Sometimes something happened.

Most times it didn't.

That was the thing with waiting for happenings, Jeepers had learned. You wouldn't know if anything was going to happen until you just sat down and waited for it to happen, or not happen, as the case might be, and he just didn't know if tonight was the kind of sometime when something would happen.

Well, it just so happened that Constance Croonstopper was out for her evening walk.

"Hey, Jeepers Magoo," she said, walking up the drive to the porch. She was sweet on Jeepers, but it was a decidedly unreciprocated sentiment.

She liked using both his names whenever she spoke to him because she thought he liked it. (He did not.) And she smelled like Scotch pine because she slept in one every night.

"You aren't waiting up for me, are you?" she asked.

"Maybe yes, maybe no... " drawled Jeepers. A hopeful smile crept up on Constance's face. "... but no. I sure wasn't." he concluded. But before Jeepers could fully enjoy crushing her spirit, the sound of loud, over-modulated yodeling reached them from somewhere around the bend.

A rusted '57 Chevy Belair with red racing stripes, tinted windows and giant stereo speakers bolted to the roof roared into view. It screeched to a crooked halt at the end of the drive, missing the mailbox by half an inch.

The driver's side door opened, and a sasquatch wearing a kilt and a vintage Charlie's Angels t-shirt emerged and ran up to them.

"Oh, not again," tsked Constance, hiding a smile behind her hands. "He wants to fight you for me," she said, cheeks blushing. And then, winking conspiratorially, she whispered: "I want you to win."

Well, without so much as a how-do-you-do, Jeepers watched as the sasquatch hoisted Constance up over his shoulder and ran her back to his car. He kicked the trunk open, threw her in, and slammed it shut.

The sasquatch then got back in the driver's seat, slammed the door, and turned the yodeling stereo up louder. He threw the car in neutral and stomped on the gas. Thick, black smoke gathered under the wheel wells and drifted across the yard, and he leaned out the window to glare at Jeepers, his eyes narrowing to yellow darts.

The tweeter on one of his speakers blew out and caught fire.

The sasquatch popped the clutch and peeled away, leaving two lines of flame behind him. "You better recogniiiize...!" he hollered, throwing up a sign of the horns as he, his burning speaker, and Constance-in-the-trunk faded off into the distance.

Jeepers puzzled over the events of the past few moments, and whether they were the something for which he'd been waiting to happen. And as the evening's calm descended on his property once again, he finally had to admit that he didn't think so.

Fireflies returned to jitterbug across the lawn, their semaphore dance syncopating against the twilight symphony of frogs, chirping as they fed on water skimmers in the pond across the road.

He was about to call it a night, when a

flying saucer about the size of loveseat dropped directly onto his mailbox from the sky. As it burst into flames, two small, giggling purple men emerged from the fuselage, animatedly warbling and twittering at each other in a series of high-pitched squeaks and clicks.

It seemed clear to Jeepers they might be drunk, and as they dropped their pants and began peeing a foamy and apparently flame-retardant urine on the fire, he frowned.

This wasn't the something for which he'd been waiting to happen, either. "But it'll do," he thought, as he reached under the swing for his shotgun.

The Kinsmen Charity Picnic, 1919

Dearest Harl,

I regret to have been several months in composing this letter, but I am headstrong, and it has taken this spot of time for my sister, Philadria Tallyburton, (you will remember her as your sister-in-law) to convince me that her counsel on the matter is wise, and good, and true.

As you know I spent a great deal of The Great War as a nurse at the front, attending to many wounded and dying soldiers, and I'm afraid the experience has left me quite shell-shocked and facing some difficulty readjusting to normal life after the war. I am at times taken by fits of disquietude and flights of fancy and I'm afraid you saw me at my worst.

Notwithstanding my condition, it is still my clear and present duty to offer you the sincerest, humblest and more unreserved of apologies for the less than desirable quality of my companionship at the Kinsmen Charity Picnic on Queen Victoria Day.

To explain further, you see, as you offered your hand to me for a dance, I saw you not as Harl Tallyburton. Rather, I imagined you as an apparition of The German Kaiser wearing a flaming beehive for a helmet and a dinner jacket made of live voles.

My memories of what transpired next are fleeting and scant, but I was nothing short of distressed to learn that I had bitten off your left eyebrow.

I am told by mutual friends that the lack of brow over your eye causes you no small amount of embarrassment. Therefore, please accept my gift of this wide-brimmed hat, and my invitation to the Lions Club Dominion Day Luncheon.

Very truly yours, with remorse most earnest,
Cedia Strongmere,
Your Admirer

PS: I have entreated upon a former field doctor colleague of mine in the neighbouring county, and he feels with some amount of confidence that it may not yet be too late to reattach the eyebrow. If indeed I did not ingest it, has it been found? Something to consider. Sincerely, Cedia.

PPS: I am, of course, bound by honour to pay for any expenses incurred in this or any procedure, should you wish to embark upon it. Regards, Cedia.

PPPS: He has also had great success in tinting and dying chipmunk tails in fashionable hues and facial hair styles, and grafting them to the upper lips of unfortunate veterans whose moustaches were blown off in battle. Another option, perhaps? Again, my treat. C.S.

Addendum: Ever so eager to hear of your decision re: Lions Day, as there is a fee incurred for cancellation. C.

The Duck on the Dock

On a fine summer day, on the shores of Bella Lake, just off Billy Bear Road, a few kilometres outside Huntsville, Ontario, was a dock. Upon that dock was a red Muskoka chair, and on that chair sat a woman named Flerennifer, upon whose lap was an open book.

It was a real page-turner, and she was so engrossed that she nearly jumped when a voice hit her ears. "Hey, you gonna eat that?"

She looked up, startled. She looked around.

Nothing.

Everybody else was still up at the cottage. That was odd. Perhaps the wind had carried a voice over to her from another dock down the lake...?

"Down here."

She looked over the edge of the pier, and down below her, floating on the lake, was a duck looking straight up at her. "Hey," repeated the duck. "You gonna eat that?"

Flerennifer wasn't sure how to respond. "Uh...? Am I gonna eat what?"

"Your book. Can I eat it?" said the duck, flapping up on the deck beside her, spraying her with water.

"You can't eat a book."

"What do *you* know? I bet they told you pumpkins can't talk, too. And yet, here I am! A talking pumpkin!"

"Who's a pumpkin?"

"Well, duh. Look at me. I'm a pumpkin, obviously."

"No, you're a duck."

The duck blinked, surprised. "I'm a *what?*"

The duck peered over the edge at his reflection... and quacked in surprise. Then, as if startled by the voice he no longer recognized, he flapped away.

Flerennifer watched him go, ashamed and saddened that she couldn't take it back, wishing for all the world she could live this moment over, and let that speaking duck lie.

The Incident

The word had gone out less than an hour ago: the bosses were making a rare visit to the lab. The legendary co-founders of ChungMorp ToyCo™ had rarely been seen, and their names only whispered in hushed tones, following... the incident.

According to protocol, non-essential personnel immediately shut down their workstations and left for the day. A clean-up team had scrubbed and disinfected every surface. The old oxygen was pumped out, and the new, imported Bavarian oxygen was pumped in. All this had been done in less than twelve minutes (breaking previous records set during rehearsal drills) and now, the twelve department heads stood at attention in a precise row by the hypervator doors.

All eyes were fixed on the blinking red indicator light above doors that signaled the steady progress of their leader, as his private box descended from the executive penthouse.

After several moments, a low, metallic tone chimed.

The airlock engaged, and the doors slid slowly open. A thick, cloying bank of fog drifted out, slinking into every nook and crevice, around every leg and against every nostril on the floor.

Silence.

Then a motorized Victorian pram carrying Enzo Chung and Shabinder Morp puttered out onto the laboratory floor.

The executives struggled to tamp down silent screams building up behind fake smiles.

Others stifled gags or averted their eyes.

The new Head of Design shit himself.

To describe them as "gruesome" would be only too polite. Chung and Morp were less than human now; they would be more accurately described as a snarling, drooling, cybernetic, double-headed flesh-bag spider-thing. But the awful procedure rendering them thus was the only thing that had kept them alive after... the incident.

The incident... had occurred during the testing phase of what Chung and Morp had believed would become their most famous and successful creation. But in their haste to rush their gadget into production, there had been some minor miscalculations with major consequences, and they themselves had born the tragic brunt.

But today, the executive team had been assured that those miscalculations had finally been rectified; with the bugs worked out, their new and improved toy would take its rightful place beside Rubik's Cube, above the Slinky, kitty-corner to the hula hoop, where it would crush the throat of the frisbee under its boot.

"Let usss begin," hissed Chung and Morp, barely intelligibly, through their shared mouth hole.

But before the assembled team could move towards the testing chamber, two huge doors at the far end of the floor burst open with a resounding crash, as a young woman came through them. "Please! Wait!" she cried, and began running towards them at full speed.

"Who daressss...?" Chung hissed (or one of them did, anyway, it was difficult to tell) through their secondary shared blowhole.

"I'm Pewny!" she panted at the top of her lungs as she covered the distance. "... I'm the intern...! From marketing...!"

An audible groan rose from the ranks. Chung raised a baleful eyebrow as Morp seethed and drooled in anger as Pewny raced to close the distance.

"... so sorry..." she wheezed, leaning against the pram to catch her breath. "... had to run... up fourteen flights of stairs... had to tell you... they said I had one job... and I really need this credit..."

Pewny looked around at the somber and frightened faces of the executive team, then into the grey pile of hair, teeth, and bodily secretions that was the company president.

She swallowed audibly.

"Only, you see," she continued. "The product is not testing well with tweens and single moms. We recommend..." and here she paused, perhaps realizing only now how precarious her position was. "With all due respect, sir... we recommend... a little more time."

Chung and Morp's three rows of transplanted, oozing spider-eyes popped and grew to twice their size as they stared unblinkingly at this young wisp of a girl. "And they sssent you here to tell me thisss..?"

"Yes, sir," said Pewny.

"I sssee," glowered Chung and Morp.

And then they said nothing for a very long time.

Unable to bear the suspense, the new Head

of Design calmly walked to the service elevator doors, pried them open with his bare hands, and threw himself down the shaft without a word.

Finally Chung and Morp spoke. "And what doesss..." He very nearly spat out the next word. "*marketing*... sssuggest we do now?"

Pewny bit her lower lip and thought. "Well... they didn't say, but I thought maybe... like... put a viral video on social media while we do more testing?"

The air went out of the room.

Chung and Morp began howling and thrashing around their pram in an absolute rage.

Windows shattered.

Huge cracks appeared in the concrete beneath their feet.

The executives leaned against the walls and each other for support. Then:

"Fine!" bellowed Chung, resignedly.

The rumbling and swaying ceased.

Loose objects that had been levitated fell smashing to the ground.

Spent from their shared psychic tantrum, Morp fell into a fitful, drooling daze, as he always did. But Chung was still very much awake, and he was still very unhappy with the turn of events.

"Everyone who isss not named Pewny, leave usss," said Chung. "Pewny, accompany usss to

our office. We would know more of thisss...
sssocial media."

The executive team scattered in every
direction, and Pewny began babbling in relief
as she followed them to the elevator. "Oh, cool,
because yeah, my boyfriend is a film-maker, and
he does these great viral videos with his sketch
troupe... They just graduated from their classes
at The Second City... "

And as they shot up to his penthouse office,
Pewny continued to chatter on about her insights
on trends, engagement and influencers.

"You are unwissse to lead her to our nesssst,"
said Morp to Chung, telepathically.

"Office," corrected Chung.

"Officcccce. Ssssorry," Morp replied. "Are you
sssure she will not turn on usss..?"

"I am not," replied Chung. "But what choice
have we? We are old. We are grotesque. But we
musssst prevail. The youngling may yet prove of
great use to usss, and at the very least, we have a
new tessst sssubject for our new and improved
'Badgerang'™."

"Yesss..." thought Morp, smiling broadly now
at Pewny (purely a muscle memory gesture at this
point, but it always caused Chung to flatulate in
D minor). "It will be magnificent. Barring any
further... incident, of coursssse..."

Gordan, Manitoba, 1969

For months, the town of Gordan, Manitoba had planned a fantastic Canada Day weekend, the highlight of which would be their first ever municipal fireworks display.

But at a town hall meeting on June 28, Mayor Clayton Dirge was forced to announce that the fireworks had to be cancelled. "It seems Ernton Derwillk over there has bought all the fireworks from here to Red Deer for himself, and he won't share."

From the second floor gallery, widower Ernton Derwillk stood to a round of boos. Nobody in this town liked him, and the feeling was mutual.

"Baaah!" he snarled, banging his cane at the assembled townspeople till they quieted down. "No, sir. I ain't sharin'. I bought all them fireworks for me, and they're for me!" And with that, he turned on his heels and stormed out, followed by catcalls, jeers and a chorus of "would you believes" and "who does he think he is's".

The children of Gordan cried themselves to sleep that night.

But adversity and a cause always brings out the best in people, and throughout the night, calls were made. Committees were struck. By the end of the following day, the well-to-do Gordanites had organized carpools and rides for each other; the entire town of Gordan (except Ernton) was going to Winnipeg for their Canada Day celebrations that year. And that suited Ernton just fine.

Just after sunrise on July 1st, after feeding the chickens, Ernton sat on a riding mower at the edge of his property. Through his binoculars, he watched the last busload of townsfolk turn off Main Street towards the highway. He threw the mower into gear and finished mowing his lawn.

Then he went inside and had a humble breakfast of porridge and coffee.

Afterwards, he let the dog out the back screen door.

He did half a crossword puzzle while having half a conversation with a picture of Mildred, his widow, who hung on the wall next to the table, just above where she used to sit.

After washing the dishes, he turned on the

radio, then went outside and sat on the porch.

Lunchtime came and went. He didn't feel hungry, so he opted instead to go inside and take a nap on the couch.

Around four o'clock, Ernton awoke to the sound of the dog whining and scratching at the screen door, so he let him in and gave him a huge bowl of dog food. He still wasn't really feeling hungry, but Ernton made himself a sandwich and took it out to the porch to eat.

And there he sat for the next four hours, watching the long shadows of the afternoon creep forward, stretching vainly to touch things they hadn't been able to reach yesterday, only to have their hopes dashed for yet another day as the sun fell below the horizon.

By now the cat was meowing at the door to be let out, so Ernton obliged. He called to the dog, who thumped his tail at him but seemed quite intent on sticking it out for the evening in the comfort of his basket by the woodstove. "Suit yourself," said Ernton, leaving the door ajar in case old Blue changed his mind.

And then, as the moon rose over the horizon, and the heat sighed and rose off the summer lawn into the cool embrace of night, Derwillk grabbed his cane and made his way out to the barn.

There, the barn owls watched him put on his

one-piece snowsuit, work gloves, scuba tank and visor. Then, he climbed up the wooden ladder to the hayloft, where he sat on the conveyor belt and rode it to the top of the grain silo adjacent to the barn.

He felt a slight twinge of regret that he'd been so headstrong and proud, and that nobody would be here to witness the fulfilment of his boyhood dream. But, he knew nobody would understand it, and worse, they'd have tried to talk him out of it.

Strapping himself into the tractor seat welded to the silo top plate, Derwillk paused for a moment. He'd long ago stopped believing in God, but as he took in the beauty and expanse of the Milky Way above him, he felt gratitude for whatever forces had made the universe, this planet, and him.

Tonight, he would touch the stars, as he always had known he would.

But a grain silo full of fireworks is significantly unlike an Apollo rocket in several critical ways.

The starburst was seen as far as Moose Jaw, and Ernton's ashes eventually covered three counties.

The Animals

Galifty Yankovic knew every winding turn on River Road like the back of her hand, which is why she'd been driving too fast when the racoon darted out of the woods in front of her.

For a brief moment she saw the poor little guy freeze on the spot, shielding his eyes against the harsh, blinding light as she bore down on him. Instinctively, Galifty clenched her teeth and oversteered to avoid running him over; left, but then much too sharply right, and despite stomping on the brakes, she was unable to stop her Volkswagen Beetle from careening off the road, over the embankment and down a steep incline into the woods.

Strangely, she wondered if she had turned the stove off.

She white-knuckled the steering wheel as the car pitched and lurched; branches, leaves and brambles slapped a backbeat at the windshield, rear-view mirrors and fenders, keeping time in an eccentric, freeform jazz rhythm.

She wondered if the police report would include the detail that she was listening to a pirated cassette copy of *The Wizard of Oz* soundtrack when she'd died.

Seconds later (though it had seemed to go on much longer) she came to a slow, gentle stop at the bottom of the hill.

She sat there a moment, then realized she had stopped breathing. She breathed in several short, sharp bursts of air, as small points of light danced in her field of vision. "Don't hyperventilate," she thought. "Don't go into shock. You're fine, you're fine."

She forced herself to take slower breaths and tried not to think about anything. Only when she'd calmed down and was reasonably certain she wasn't going to pass out did she click off the stereo, just as the Lollipop Guild were welcoming Dorothy to Munchkinland.

A few moments later, she got out of the car and inspected the damage.

The driver's side rear-view was gone. The car was dented and scratched to hell and one headlight was hanging by wires like a droopy eye from a socket, but despite it all, the damn thing was still running, and she counted her blessings.

However, once back in the car, after several attempts to rock it back and forth to free herself, she'd only succeeded in sinking deeper into the soft, muddy earth. There was no way she was driving back to the top of the hill now. She was stuck.

A thorough search through her pockets and then the entire car (even under the seats) confirmed that she'd forgotten her cellphone at home, so she wasn't going to call for help, either.

Supposing it was best to just climb back up to the road in the hopes that someone would drive by, Galifty was about to take her keys out of the ignition when she saw them.

A dozen or so animals had gathered in a moon-dappled semi-circle around the front of her car, their blazing eyes fixed on hers. Galifty gulped audibly and locked her doors.

Step by step, they approached the car, teeth bared, hackles raised, closing the distance until their breath was steaming up her windows...

And then... the unimaginable happened.

First, the black bear leaned in against the grille, his huge back paws slipping till his claws found purchase. With one, two, three huge rocking shoves, he'd pushed the car a solid foot out of the mud.

Within moments a half-dozen rabbits jumped in to push against the fenders.

Then, a number of possums, squirrels, a lynx (or was it a bobcat, Galifty wasn't sure) had joined a pack of wolves, a moose, and a deer. Every paw, head, talon, butt and antler pushed and heaved as inch by inch, foot by foot, the car began to roll up the hill.

Galifty's mouth was agape, and even more so when a squadron of bats flew overhead, holding fireflies gently in their mouths, lighting the motley crew's path back up the hill.

It took nearly twenty breathless minutes, and when the animals had slowly but surely returned Galifty and her car safely back up to the road, they turned and walked, scampered, flew, slunk or sauntered back into the woods.

Breathlessly, Galifty got out of the car. "Wait," she called out into the night. "I... thank you!"

There was no response.

She walked to the side of the road and looked down into the darkness, as tears welled up in her eyes. She was filled with gratitude and wonder; with the idea that, even at the subatomic level, every being, every entity, every point of consciousness in the universe was all one thing, one continuity, one wonderful family of stardust...

It was then that she heard the car door slam.

Whirling, she saw her Volkswagen filled boot to bonnet with fur and fauna. The engine revved, slapped into gear, and her car lurched off into the night.

The animals were heading to town. And she could have sworn the raccoon riding the back fender had given her the finger.

Not Working

She'd lost her job, dumped her boyfriend, and was sick with a cold that would not go away, so you'll understand why Megun Thwap woke up that day an emotional wreck.

The new medication her therapist had prescribed was not working because, unbeknownst to her, it was a placebo, because he felt what she was going through was situational, rather than the result of any chemical imbalance. So she popped another useless tablet that was not working, hoping it would calm her down.

Rather than try and face another grey morning she decided to just try and get more sleep, so she also popped some melatonin and went back to bed.

An hour later, it was evident the melatonin was not working.

Megun flopped out of bed, into grey sweats

and Birkenstocks and trudged to the kitchen to make a coffee. With water poured into the carafe, she hit the switch and then stared through her living room and out at the balcony.

For a long time.

Then, shaking herself out of it, she realized that the water in her coffee maker hadn't started dripping into the carafe. Flipping the switch on and off did nothing, and pulling out the plug from the wall in frustration rewarded her with a spray of sparks from the socket.

Great.

The coffee maker was not working.

Still needing caffeine, Megun opted for the half-can of flat cola she'd left on the counter a few days ago. She'd tried to save the fizz in it by covering the top with tin foil. Turns out that trick had not worked, but she didn't care. She riffled through the cupboards and found a bag of stale chips and trudged back to the living room. She hunted for the remote between the cushions and couldn't find it.

She looked under the couch.

Nope.

It wasn't in the bathroom, either.

She found it, finally, right out in the open in front of the television where she'd left it the night before. She grabbed it and flipped on the

TV over her shoulder as she returned to the couch for a sip of flat cola.

Static.

Channel after channel she was treated to nothing but static.

The cable was not working.

Frustrated, Megun walked over to the den and sat down petulantly at the computer so she could tweet how crappy Rogers Cable was.

hey @rogerscable suck much #notworking

She hit tweet... once, twice... and nothing happened, because looking at the top right hand of her screen, she saw now that her internet was not working.

"Oh, internet!" she moaned. "Why you no working?"

She knew why; her internet was not working because she hadn't paid the bills in several months, because she was also not working. It was a vicious circle and she felt very much the victim, more worked against than not working.

Overcome with self-pity, she stomped out of the den and fell to the floor in the throes of a good old fashioned tantrum, thrashing and wailing and gnashing and flailing, and then, as she ran out of steam, Megun grew quiet and turned over onto her side, looking down the hall again towards the balcony.

For a long time.

Her fingers and toes were freezing, yet she felt a little warm; she thought maybe she was feverish, or more likely, just dehydrated? She remembered she had half a bottle of soda water, so off to the fridge she went, only to find it had stopped working. The fridge smelled of things going sour, and her soda water was not only just room temperature, but flat.

She walked to her hallway closet, grabbed a hammer and returned to beat the shit out of the fridge. Afterwards, she tossed the hammer to the floor and walked back to stand in front of the balcony door.

She stood there, arms crossed, gazing out at the blue sky.

For a long time.

No.

She had to distract herself.

She knew that a good walk with a good podcast always made her feel better. She went over to her night table to find her phone, but realized she hadn't plugged it in overnight, and the battery was dead.

Even her iPhone wasn't working!

It was too much to bear, and finally, tired of distracting herself with one dead-end option after another, Megun walked straight to the balcony door, and opened it.

She pushed the patio chair up against the ledge, using it as a step-ladder to climb up.

Then she took a deep breath, and stepped off into nothing.

She plunged twelve stories to the sidewalk.

After which Megun stood up, completely uninjured, happy that the sidewalk wasn't working today, either.

Can of Beans

Grajomelie Knerb opened her pantry door and noticed – just in front of the usual kitcheny paraphernalia on the top shelf – a small tin can with no label that had not been there the day before.

"Strange," she thought, for thinking in one-word thoughts was in fact her forte.

She had no recollection of ever 'buying', 'owning' or 'storing' this 'can'.

She took the can in her 'hand' and examined "it" carefully.

On the bottom, in handwriting that was not her own, she read just one word, written in permanent marker:

BEANS

"Can," she thought, because her second strongest forte was the art of missing a beat or two and falling a step behind in the narrative.

"Beans," she thought, finally catching up.

She puzzled over this can of beans a few more moments, which gave her brain time to conjure (her third forte) the fact that she possessed an 'opener'.

"Drawer," she said, walking to the drawer.

"Open," she said, opening the drawer.

"Opener," she said, taking out the opener and giggling to herself a little, because repetition is funny.

She climbed onto the counter on all fours (she did her best can-opening that way) and positioned the can lip against the cutting edge of the opener. She applied pressure, puncturing the can, and then twisted the 'handle' to watch the can go 'around'.

But upon lifting the lid, instead of finding "beans" as she had anticipated, she found a probability wave, which replaced her in that exact time and moment with Schrödinger's meerkat. With his forepaws on the opener, he had an initially triumphant expression on his face, till the reality of his situation set in.

He was crestfallen; once again, despite all his calculations, his eternity in the aether had borne him neither an opposable thumb or the meal of beans he so desperately craved. And he'd been so close.

He hissed and sprayed in frustration, then leapt directly into the sink to hide.

Molly's Ex

Molly and Jason were on their third date, sharing a deep-dish margherita at a cozy corner table at *PizzazziPer*, when a scowling, grungy man walked in carrying a pizza box.

He wore dark robes, an obviously fake moustache and a faux-fur hipster hat. As he walked past their table on his way to the take-out counter, he pretended not to notice them sitting there, but cleared his throat to make himself noticed, so they would look up to see him pretending not to notice them.

Molly shielded her face and sank down a bit in her seat.

Jason noticed Molly's reaction. "You know that guy?" he asked, turning to look.

"He's nobody," Molly said, sinking lower in her seat.

The dark robed man walked up to the counter at the back of the room where he slammed the pizza down. "I'm returning this pizza. The order's all wrong," he barked at the meek and pimply cashier. "I asked for extra figs!"

"Sorry about that, sir," replied the cashier. "We can fix that right away." He grabbed the under-figged pizza and scurried back to the kitchen with it. "I should think so," growled the boorish customer. He then picked up a menu and opened it, pretending to read from it as he threw dark, belligerent glances in Molly and Jason's direction.

"We should go," said Molly, grabbing Jason's arm and pulling him towards the door.

"Okay, uh, sure..." said Jason, off balance and struggling to grab his jacket off the back of the chair. "Wanna get the food boxed to go, maybe?"

But it was too late. Out of the corner of her eye, Molly saw the man waggle a finger in their direction. Jason stopped dead in his tracks. His eyes bulged. The colour drained from his cheeks, and his forehead burrowed in concern as a bounty of locusts, snakes and a single barn owl exploded from Jason's mouth, nose and anus.

"Jason, I'm so sorry," said Molly.

Without another word, Jason left the restaurant as the creatures swarmed, writhed and wriggled their way out of the dining room.

Molly's shoulders slumped, and she returned

to her seat and sat down. By this point, the cashier had returned from the kitchen with a freshly figged pizza. "Here you go, sir." He rang up the register and gave the man a handful of cash. "This was on us, so no charge for the pizza. Sorry about the inconvenience."

"Thank you," sneered the man, snatching the money from his hand. "And there will be no gratuity." Then he turned to leave with his pizza, but with an exaggerated double take, feigned surprise at seeing Molly sitting there.

"Wha... Molly? Is that you?" he said, walking over to her. "Well, hi... What are you doing here?"

"Hello, The Warlock..." sighed Molly, resignedly. "You are a complete and utter prick."

"Hmn. Yes. Well. You still have my Fleetwood Mac album."

Molly gritted her teeth and slammed her hands together. A ball of crackling green and blue lightning bolts danced around her clenched fist. "Rumours... is... mine!" she hissed, discharging the blast squarely into The Warlock's chest. He flew backwards out of his hat, landing in a crumpled heap on top of the jukebox.

"Hey, what's going on here?!" yelled the cashier, running out from the kitchen, just as the barn owl alighted on Molly's shoulder and rubbed her head affectionately against her cheek.

"Hello, Chrona," she said, tickling her under the chin. "I missed you, too."

"Miss, you can't have owls in here," said the cashier. Molly walked past The Warlock as he groaned and came to. "Too bad you don't have the same rule about assholes," she said, walking out the door with Chrona.

The Warlock groaned and sat up, holding his head. "You okay, dude?" asked the cashier.

"Shut up, you imbecile," snapped The Warlock.

"You're an imbecile," muttered the cashier.

"What did you say to me?" said The Warlock as a ball of fire gathered in his clenched fist. The cashier blanched. "Say it again. I dare you."

As they squared off, The Warlock's fake moustache, already hanging at a weird angle, fell to the floor.

The cashier blinked in recognition. "Hey!" he said. "I know you! You can't be in here! We told you last week, you're banned for life from this location!"

"Ban this, cashier!" shrieked The Warlock as he unleashed his fireball. To his surprise, the cashier lifted his hand, stopping the fireball a foot from his face, where it sputtered and sparked impotently in mid-air like a dog at the end of its chain.

"That's Mister Cashier to you, jerk," sneered the cashier, shooting the fireball back at The Warlock's crotch, at twice the speed. "Magico cullus loco vices!" he said, instantly transporting The Warlock to the *PizzazziPer* location across town.

"For fucks sake!" said a voice from the kitchen.

The cashier turned to see the chef scowling at him. "You, too? Christ, is everybody but me and Jason some sort of fuckin' magician in this town?"

Two Hikers

O nce upon a time, two hikers went for a
hike in the woods. By 'once upon a time',
I mean last week, and by 'hike in the woods', I
mean hike in the woods.

Anyway, it was a beautiful day, birds were
chirping, and there wasn't a cloud in the sky,
and by that I mean there were in fact several
clouds, but despite this, the two hikers, who
were nonsexual friends, were having a great day.

By 'nonsexual friends', I mean they had never
had sexual relations with each other (or anybody
else, for that matter) and by 'great day', I mean
the sort of day as great as you would expect to get
in a life that had been sexless to that point.

Anyway, they were sharing the sort of stories
you might share if you were sexless and hiking,
when a sudden noise made one of the hikers a
bit suspicious.

And by 'suspicious', I mean, the following

discussion then happened:

"Did you just fart?"

"No."

"Really?"

"Yeah."

"You didn't just fart?"

"No."

"But I heard you."

"No, you didn't."

"Yes, I did."

"You did not."

"I say you did, because I heard it."

"No, you didn't, because I didn't!"

"You did!"

"I didn't!"

"So what was that noise that came out of your ass?"

"Drop it."

"Why?"

"Just drop it. It's none of your business."

"I thought we were friends."

"We are."

"So, if we're friends, why are you making such a big deal about farting in front of me? What's a fart among friends?"

"Because I didn't fart!"

"Then what was that sound I heard coming out of your ass?!"

"It's a bear."

"What?"

"I have a bear in my ass."

"That's ridiculous."

"What's ridiculous?"

"That you would claim to have a bear in your ass."

"Well, thanks for the sensitivity. Some friend you turned out to be."

"What are you talking about?"

"I guess that'll teach me to be vulnerable again."

"Vulnerable? About what?!"

"About the bear in my ass! I've never told anybody about it. That was a very hard thing for me to admit to you!"

"You do not have a bear in your ass."

"I do so have a bear in my ass."

"Bullshit. You farted!"

"I didn't fart."

"You farted and you're trying to blame it on having a bear in your ass."

"I did not fart."

"What's the big deal admitting you farted?"

"I just don't like being forced to admit to something I didn't do."

"So you'd rather blame it on something like having a bear in your ass."

"I don't like the tone of your voice."

"There was no tone."

"I heard tone."

"And there's no bear, either. You farted."

"I didn't fart."

"You farted, and you're embarrassed to admit it, and that's fine, you don't have to admit it. I'll drop it right now. But you do not have a bear in your ass."

"Let me ask you this, then, you're so smart; have you ever, and I mean, ever, met anybody who claimed to have a bear in his ass?"

"This would be the first time."

"So, who would make something like that up?"

"You might."

"Why would I do that?"

"You might do that because you're embarrassed about having farted in front of me."

"Well, I wouldn't be, and I didn't."

"So what was that noise I heard?"

"I think what you heard was the bear in my ass."

"You do not have a bear in your ass!"

"Yes I do have a bear in my ass!"

"Prove it."

And then the hiker with the bear in his ass let it out, and that bear mauled the first sexless hiker. And that's why hikers always say "Beware letting the bear out of your ass, lest it maul your hiking partner."

.

Champs-Élysées

As he sat sipping his fourth café au lait du jour on his favourite patio along the Champs-Élysées, Monsieur Shnafp Flaubert Montpassant-Duflânche engaged in his favourite pastime; that of hating people.

With its cinemas, cafés, luxury specialty shops and clipped horse-chestnut trees, this was the perfect milieu from which to "regardez" the parade of peoples from across the world, and "detester tout le monde."

"Tout le monde" could not miss him, either, for when passersby were foolhardy enough to meet his sang-froid gaze directly, he would fling a hard, stale croissant at their heads and curse them out loud.

To say that his disposition was inhospitable was an understatement, for the very air within two feet of Monsieur Montpassant-Duflânche grew damp and cold. He had a decidedly pale complexion, with ruddy blue lips, steel-grey eyes and a walking cane made from solid sneers. No matter how many café au lait he drank, he was always 'froid', drawing his fur coat tighter, shivering as he blew into one of a series of seemingly endless woven handkerchiefs he kept in his pockets and sleeves.

A fixture at *Café Qui-Est-La* for as long as anyone remembered, he would leave as the café closed, returning only when the 'ouvert' sign turned over the next morning. He ran a tab but paid promptly on the last day of every month – to the franc and not one centime more. The staff had begun to think of him as something of their own personal gargoyle; terrible to look at, worse to interact with, but if he kept the bad luck and evil spirits away, c'est la vie.

One day, after seeing him ding yet another passing croissant-worthy tourist in the temple, a new waitress named Genevieve approached him and boldly asked the unimaginable:

"Pourquoi?"

At that precise moment, coffee in the café stopped dripping.

Milk and cream curdled in their bottles.

A champagne bottle uncorked itself through the stained glass window above the door.

Clocks all along the *Champs* stopped.

A murder of crows on the wing flew into the Arc de Triomphe and fell stunned and twitching to the ground.

The entire arrondissement seemed to grind to a halt.

The old man turned to look at her with the most perfectly puzzled expression on his face.

"Pourquoi?" he repeated, his voice rough as sandpaper. Genevieve was frozen to the spot.

"Pourquoi?" He turned the word over in his mind as his eyes bored into hers.

Then, he replied.

"Pourquoi pas?"

And in that moment, all his memories, dreams, disappointments, triumphs, loves and heartaches poured from him into her, a maelstrom of regret and chagrin, a lifetime of things left unsaid, and things that could never be unsaid.

She gasped, nearly doubled over, and leant on him for support, her eyes never leaving his. And together, they wept silently, he in gratitude, and she in a state of non-Parisian empathy she had never experienced, and was ill-equipped to comprehend.

A Debate with My Eyeballs

I was in an eastbound 504 King streetcar, having a debate with my eyeballs about the merits of getting a better look at what I thought we had just seen down the aisle.

"Look again..." I told them.

"Mind your business," my eyes replied. "It could be something you cannot unsee."

I frowned. They had a point. I really *should* mind my own business. This was Toronto, after all, a vibrant Canadian city whose two main exports were a kind of self-apathy, combined with the almost universal contempt its very existence engendered in the rest of the nation.

"But I've seen it," I told my eyes. "Sort of. Anyway, I'm not sure if I actually saw what I think I saw."

"So?"

Not counting myself or the driver who was minding his business, there was one other person

75

left on the streetcar, so I ignored my advising eyes, put on my best liar's face, and looked "randomly" towards the other passenger... and then down at his...

I stared. Yes. I saw it. Uh huh. And there it was.

"Told you so," said my eyes. As if he'd heard them, the man turned and glanced towards me, and instead of looking away, I looked up.

Our eyes locked.

We both visibly jumped.

"Your mouth is open," said my eyes. They were right again, of course.

To compensate, I feigned covering a yawn; a sort of jerky, maladroit theatrical grotesquerie as would hurt even a very bad mime's feelings. My ruse might have worked had my Judas-eyes not remained locked with his the whole time.

"You're staaaaaring," I told my eyes.

"We knoooow," they replied. "Now we can't look awaaaay. We tooooold you soooo..."

I blinked my eyelids shut, and rolled my head in what I hoped was a credible range of motion towards the window. "Okay, eyelids, you got this. Be casual."

Instead, my eyelids snapped open very not casually at all, with a bit of a liquid pop, and much, much wider than necessary, forcing my eyebrows to settle at an unnaturally high position on my forehead, conveying not nonchalance as was called for, but rather a sort of awkward, twitching upper-facial palsy.

Peripherally, I could tell the man was still staring at me. I'd really need to do some work to sell this, so I slid open my window to wave and yell "Steve! Hi, Steve!" at a passing stranger.

The man stood up and turned to face me, his face flushed with embarrassed rage.

Storm clouds and lightning bolts gathered around his head, and it began raining inside the streetcar, drenching us all. "Yes!" he bellowed in an accent that was simultaneously Greek, Japanese and British. "Yes, I have radishes for hands!" He held them aloft and looked to the heavens, eyes clenched, tears streaming from his face now. "I HAVE RADISHES FOR HANDS!"

And with that, the indoor storm passed, and the man sadly got off at the next stop.

"See?" said my eyes.

And they were right, of course. As usual.

Hortch's Cola

Peeking over the edge of the overturned living room coffee-table into the kitchen, Hortch watched the cola can spinning on the counter, spitting molten lava and smoke. Yet another of his experiments had just backfired, and he was sure he didn't want to be near this one when it blew.

"Hortch, do something!" yelled the cat, who Hortch was quite certain had never spoken to him before – a detail he took note of, but filed under 'later'. But the cat was right, he had to do something...

There was a basket of yarn by the loveseat. Not ideal, but it would do.

He dragged himself over to the loveseat by his elbows, tossed the yarn aside and put the basket on his head. Then, he rolled over to the fireplace to grab the wood tongs. Then, taking two huge breaths and holding the third one, he ran headlong into the kitchen.

The smoke hung low from the ceiling and was now getting hard to see through, but he managed to grab the violently sparking can with the tongs. Holding them at arms length, he ran with them straight towards the balcony door.

Then he, his helmet-basket, tongs and volcanic coke can bounced off the balcony door. For all his prior experience in this step-by-step world, he had failed to remind himself that opening a glass door was indeed a mandatory prerequisite to crossing through it, no matter the relative rate of speed or need to get through it.

He was running out of time.

By this point, the can had bounced, rolled and hell-fired all the way back to the kitchen to its exact original coordinates on the kitchen counter; only NASA could have been more precise.

Hortch picked himself up, and opened the sliding glass door. He was nobody's idiot, twice.

He fished out the tongs from under the television stand where they'd slid. Then he cartwheeled into the kitchen (unnecessarily, though impressively for a man of his size), where he grabbed the can again with the tongs, and raced it back out onto his fourteenth floor balcony.

There, he threw the can-tongs-surprise down to the street below, where it fell into the open sunroof of a Nissan Sentra that happened to be driving by at the exact moment of detonation.

The blast created a singularity that swallowed the car, the sunroof, the driver, a newspaper box and the south-west part of the convenience store across the street, instantly transporting all those things and that person into the middle of a heated battle raging on the moon of Nebulon IV.

"There," said Hortch, sliding his balcony door closed. "Now it's someone else's problem. Now then, if I'm not mistaken," he said to the cat, "Someone who is not me but is in fact you was just talking. And just how long has that being going on?"

The cat's only only reply was to lick his own balls.

"Two can play at that game," Hortch thought, erroneously.

But first... to the kitchen, to see if ginger ale worked better.

The Baloney Only Rings Once, Probably

The doorbell chimed, and Ghurge Jones looked up from his paper. "That's odd," he thought, "I don't have a doorbell."

He got up with difficulty from his easy chair, and went to his door. "Huh," he said, noticing the peephole he'd never had before. "I don't have a peephole."

Looking through the peephole, he saw a delivery man in the hallway, looking at a clipboard. "Hello?" he said suspiciously.

"Baloney Delivery," said the delivery guy, without looking up from his clipboard.

"Baloney Delivery?" said Ghurge. "Do you mean bologna?"

"No." said the delivery guy impatiently.

"I didn't order any baloney," said Ghurge.

"Ghurge Jones?"

"Yes," replied Ghurge.

"Bologna Delivery, then," repeated the delivery guy, quite stridently. "I'm here to delivery your bologna."

Ghurge considered his options.

An hour passed.

Finally he opened the door.

"Was that so hard?" said the delivery guy, extending the clipboard. "Sign here, please."

"I refuse to take delivery of bologna I didn't order," said Ghurge.

The delivery guy was taken aback. "You can't do that!"

"Oh, can't I?" asked Ghurge, testing out an imperious tone he immediately regretted as it felt overly contrariant.

The delivery guy considered the question carefully. He took off his head and scratched his hat, which was a very interesting way of doing it, thought Ghurge, making a mental note to try doing it that way next time.

The delivery guy made a series of clicking and chuffing sounds, and consulted his clipboard. "Don't think so," he finally said. "Sign here."

Ghurge huffed. "Oh, alright." He signed for it, and the delivery guy gave him a single slice of baloney and turned to leave.

"What am I supposed to do with this?" he asked.

"What do I care?" said the delivery guy.

Ghurge and the baloney slice were married in a small ceremony the following year.

Shlank & Entropy

"Okay, Entropy, you kin come out. I seen ya," said Constable Grievous Shlank, shining a huge spotlight through the rain and fog from the comfort of his 1949 Plymouth police cruiser.

"No you never!" yelled Entropy from the darkness of the ditch. Cold, wet and miserable, he lay clutching a small satchel of gold teeth he'd pried from Old Lady Granchman's toughened old beak. He cursed his luck. Grave robbing was tough work, especially with Shlank around.

"You mean to tell me this ain't your shovel here in the middle of the road, Entropy?" replied Grievous.

There was silence for a moment. Then, Entropy peeked out over the edge of the ditch and saw his shovel lying there on the yellow line, clearly illuminated by the police car's headlights.

"Well, hey, there Entropy," said Grievous. "I

guess it is you, after all, eh?"

Realizing he'd sat up directly in the line of Shlank's spotlight, Entropy dove back into hiding. "Stupid, stupid!" he muttered to himself.

"Come on, now, don't make me get outta the car, Entropy," said Shlank, pulling the tab on his styrofoam coffee cup as the rain pitter-pattered on the hood. Steam rose up his nose and fogged his horn-rims. He blew into the cup a few times and gently took a sip. "Got an extra coffee for ya if you want it."

Time passed.

A burst of lightning and thunder rolled across the land, and it began to rain harder.

Grievous reached into the back seat and pulled out a blanket. He laid it out carefully over the passenger set, and then went back to his coffee.

After a few more moments, Entropy resignedly got up and trudged over to the car with his satchel. He got in on the front passenger's side with all the resentment a nineteen year-old high school dropout could muster, and stared sullenly down at his wet, muddy boots on the floor. A moment passed, and he realized Shlank was looking at him, amusedly.

"What?" snorted Entropy.

"Forget something?" asked Shlank, nodding

towards the road.

Entropy looked out the windshield at the shovel. "Fine, whatever," he muttered, and stomped out to retrieve it. He threw it into the back of the car and then shoved himself back in the passenger seat.

Shlank offered Entropy a coffee, which the young man moodily grabbed, and sipped slowly to warm himself up.

"So that's fourteen tries over six weeks," said Grievous.

"I can count!" snapped Entropy.

"Didn't say you couldn't," replied Shlank. He put the car in gear and drove four miles back to Maple Grove Cemetery, through the gates and up to Old Lady Granchman's headstone, where he put the car in park. The two continued sipping their coffees for a few moments in silence.

"Well..." said Shlank. "Looks like the rain's lifted. You know what to do, I suppose."

Entropy glared sullenly at the older man. He shoved the door open, grabbed his shovel from the back, and under the glare of the headlights, he dug the old lady back up, put her teeth back in, and then covered her up again.

Shlank then drove Entropy home. As Entropy moodily slammed the car door shut, Shlank leaned over and rolled down the passenger window.

"See you tomorrow night?" said Shlank.

"No you won't," retorted Entropy. "I'll hide better."

"Awright, then," said Shlank.

"Whatever," said Entropy.

"I'd like your permission to call on your mother one day if you say it's okay," said Shlank.

"Whatever," said Entropy. "Gross."

"Awright, then," said Shlank. "Have a good night."

Entropy said nothing. Shlank shrugged, rolled up the window and backed out of the driveway. Entropy watched the red tail fins disappear into the night.

He let himself into the house quietly, took off his boots and hung up his jacket.

He'd never fall asleep now that he'd had that coffee, and listening to the radio would be too loud and wake up his mother. So he stood there indecisively in the hallway, listening to the grandfather clock (always twelve minutes late) as it marked the slow, dull, tick-tock passage of time from the living room.

He was wasting his life.

"You have a good night," retorted Entropy at the top of his lungs, proud of himself but also annoyed he hadn't come up with it sooner, when

Shlank had actually been in the yard to hear it.

"Who's that?" came his mother's voice from upstairs. "What's going on?"

Entropy held his breath and said nothing till he thought she'd fallen back asleep. Then he crept over to the couch, rather than squeak his way up the stairs. And if she brought it up tomorrow, he'd let her think he'd just been talking in his sleep.

Maniac with a Chainsaw

Stephraliee Frmp was fond of thinking of herself as one of the nicest people she knew.

She always did her best to be considerate of others, and as she walked along the side of a wooded road on the way to her house, she heard cracking branches and became aware that someone was following her.

But instead of running away, she slowed down her pace considerably.

"You mustn't automatically assume the worst," she thought to herself. "It could just be someone who admires me, and is following me at respectful distance. Or perhaps it is someone who is lost. I shouldn't just assume that the person or thing who made that noise is a goalie-mask-wearing maniac with a chainsaw."

But it was indeed a goalie-mask-wearing maniac with a chainsaw, which she realized as soon as he thundered out of the woods, revving his chainsaw and lunging towards her maniacally.

She screamed and began running away as fast as she could. "Why me?" she thought as she ran. "I'm one of the nicest people I know!"

She continued screaming and running ever harder to her little house, surrounded on all sides by a fence with a well appointed little latch gate. She hurriedly let herself in and shut the gate behind her, just as the goalie-mask-wearing maniac with a chainsaw arrived hot on her heels.

Stephraliee ran into her house, slammed the door, and leaned against it, struggling to catch her breath.

Silence.

Timidly, she looked out the round half-moon window at the top of the door, and saw the goalie-mask-wearing maniac was just standing there, on the other side of the little gate, looking at the house.

"What is he doing?" she thought. "Why wouldn't he just open it, or chainsaw through it with his chainsaw?" she wondered.

Then she had another thought.

"Maybe he's just... polite?" Then her heart skipped a beat. "Could he be... a kindred spirit? Could he also be... one of the nicest people I know? I mean, surely a goalie-mask-wearing maniac with a chainsaw who respects a closed gate and waits politely to be invited into the yard can't be all that bad?"

And she went out, and opened the gate for the maniac.

But this maniac wasn't polite at all, after all.

He was just lazy.

And patient.

Les Griffes

"My name's Bruno and I'll be your waiter today," said Bruno, a large Kodiak bear wearing an ill-fitting tuxedo.

What Meredith and Stanley Drangler heard instead was nothing but grunts and growls, and Bruno realized his translation collar was malfunctioning... again.

"Fucking otters can't do anything right," he thought to himself, as he nervously twiddled and tweaked the control buttons on the collar, doing his best to grin and... well, bear it.

The Dranglers faces dropped. They had expected more from *Les Griffes,* and for good reason: At 11,492 feet, *Les Griffes* prided itself on being the highest elevated, most exclusive French restaurant run by wild animals in the British Columbian Rockies.

The waiting list was over a year long; longer if no one could pull strings for you. And even if those strings were pulled, physically getting to the restaurant was something of an obstacle.

Diners were expected to make their way to a remote airfield in Northern British Columbia. From there, with the barest of survival gear, and no food (the better to work up an appetite) reservation-holders were airdropped somewhere within fifty kilometres of the restaurant from a retrofitted WWII Lancaster (one of only two still flying in the world). Missing your reservation or needing a search party called out to find you resulted in immediate cancellation of your reservation, with no refund.

The Dranglers had dropped with three other couples. They themselves had fared quite well, arriving only two hours later than the Austrians, who were now well into dessert, a wonderful-looking flambe being served by an effusively attentive bobcat.

The same could not be said of the other two couples, however. The bickering Columbians' chutes had become tangled immediately, and they'd dropped like potato sacks down the face of the mountain.

The Italian couple had fared slightly better, but only by half. Mrs. Buenocolireminelli – a very mousey woman – had been attacked and carried away by owls from a competing bistro.

Her husband now sat at the bar, told he would only be seated once all members of his party arrived, consoling himself with many Comparis, and going through the mistress contact list on his phone, deleting those with whom he was no longer on speaking terms.

But now the Dranglers stared stupidly at Bruno. They were hungry and exhausted, and trying to make the best of it, but when Bruno tried to mime the specials for them a third time, Mrs. Drangler innocently requested a different waiter.

Bruno lost his bear shit.... for the third time today. He knew *Les Griffes* had an anti-mauling policy, but fuck it. He was a bear.

And he was union.

cliché and wind Go Hitchhiking

In the spring of 1959, after misinterpreting a message inside a fortune cookie, I drove eastbound from my mother's house in Winnipeg to Halifax, where I would throw a bag of my hair and a rake into the Atlantic Ocean.

At first, I reveled in the solitude of the open road.

I rejoiced in having no set schedule.

I pointed the car in whichever direction I fancied at every turn, which to my surprise led to me right by my mother's house again two hours later. She was outside watering the lawn, so I ignored her double take and hunkered down in my seat as I drove by. (We never spoke of it.)

So, after consulting an almanac and picking east as a general direction from that point forward, I resumed my trek. It was nothing but the wheel, the blacktop and me for days.

On occasion, my Campfire notebook would bid me, siren-like, to stop along the road to jot down a thought or an observation; willing my brain to bleed out some truism about suffering and the human experience through the tip of my pencil. But six days of this with nothing more than doodles and half a limerick had left me feeling a little sorry for myself. What was I doing out here?

And then, as I motored past the exit for Wallaceburg, Ontario, I saw her thumb several hundred yards down the road.

Then I saw her.

She was dressed in a gingham blouse, poodle skirt, bobby socks and saddle shoes, and as her sparkling brown eyes locked on my blue one, her smile washed over me like sunshine. She was unique in a trite sort of way, a complete stranger yet somehow familiar, and even as Ricky Nelson crooned "Poor Little Fool" from the radio (was he warning me, or slighting her?) I ignored my beating heart and pulled over.

"Hey, daddy-oh," she said as she leaned in through the passenger window. "I'm cliché." She nodded her chin towards my driver's side window. "This is wind."

I turned, and there he was smiling at me, an inch from my face.

"Oh!" I said, startled. "I'm sorry. I didn't see you earlier... uh. Hello." In reply, he blew in my ear.

"We're headed to Splitsville, daddy-oh." she said. "Think you can you get us there?"

"Splitsville, Splitsville, hmn..." I mumbled to myself, trying to stall as I unfolded a map across the driver's wheel. I'd never picked up any hitchhikers before, thinking it imprudent.

"You know you're pretty cute, for a hubcap," cliché giggled. "I'm talking Splitsville, see? Anywhere but here?"

"Oh! Splitsville!" I said, finally getting it. "You were speaking idiomatically."

"Was I?" said cliché. "You hear that, wind? I'm bilingual! Well, what'll it be, Clyde? Are you hep, or square?"

"Oh, Splitsville is where I'm headed for sure, or somewhere close to -" And with that, wind breezed over my shoulder and into the back seat, blowing the map out of my hands and up into a tree in the process.

"Let's beat feet, baby!" squealed cliché, now sitting comfortably in the passenger seat. I was frozen in confusion.

"Let's go, daddy! Lay a patch! Burn rubber, beakel," she continued till I caught her "drift", and so I stomped on the accelerator, leaving two lines of smoldering caoutchouc behind me.

"Wow! What a hot rod!" she whooped, throwing her hands in the air as if she was riding a roller-coaster. A whistle of pain came from the back seat. I looked back to see wind throwing a red hot rod out the window.

"Sorry, wind," I said. "I don't know how that got back there." But wind was unruffled; he just winked at me in the rear-view and blew on his burnt fingers. I blushed with excitement; the juxtaposition of literal and figurative was a thunderclap unlike anything I'd ever experienced before.

"This ride is cherry," said cliché, looking over the interior of the car. "What'll she do?"

"She'll do this," I said, shoulder-checking while using my signal light, before stepping harder on the gas to execute an impetuous crawl into the passing lane, for no good reason as there were no other cars on this stretch of road. Giddy with adrenaline, and anxious to impress, I grinned at her stupidly.

"You're kookie," she said. "But that's cool. We're a bit kookie, too, ain't we, wind?"

But wind ignored her. He was busily blowing clouds of dandelion seeds around the interior of the car. Which was strange, as dandelions weren't going to be in season for several more weeks.

"Oh, I love the music in these new cars," said cliché, and without so much as asking if I would mind, began punching selector buttons till she found the exact frequency of garbled static she wanted and left it there. She then began rooting through her large handbag.

"You're stuck between stations," I offered after a few moments. "But I'm sure there's a CBC affiliate somewhere on th—"

"Shh, baby," she said, putting a finger to my mouth. "You're so much more interesting when you're quiet." She then applied eyeshadow above my right eye.

My memories of the next few days are scant and blurry, stuck together like pages of an old sun-faded, water-damaged magazine, with some vivid exceptions:

———————————————

While wind leaned over the seat between us and gently tousled my hair, she recited several poems she had memorized that she claimed were "unpublished first drafts" she had sold to Allen Ginsberg. I began to reconsider having opened myself up to these freewheelers and their bohemian ways, to new ideas and poems that didn't seem to rhyme. Or have a point. Or an ending...

She played a pair of bongos, while wind made a game of pulling newspapers into my face through the window. I was now wishing them both dead in that privately contemptuous but outwardly pleasant façade which was my Canadian birthright.

While she read my palm, wind gradually stretched and pulled my lips back till they flapped like a basset hound's. I fantasized about the the savagely worded note of reproach I would mail them one day.

In an attempt to ditch them at a roadside gas bar, I gave them money and sent them to the canteen to buy food, but when I hurriedly returned from paying for gas, they were already sitting back in the car. They were sharing a chocolate sundae, and since I hadn't said what I wanted, cliché had brought me a packet of ketchup and cup of hot water. "They give you these free. You can make some tomato soup if you want," she said. "Was there any change?" I asked. "Sure," she said, and tuned the radio to another squelchy frequency.

At some point wind had hung a pair of

fuzzy dice from the rear-view mirror. He would intermittently burst out from any possible corner to bat the dice like a crazed thing, only to disappear under the seat, frightening me out of my wits each time. "You're a riot, wind, a living riot!" laughed cliché, finding this unendingly hilarious. "Riot rhymes with quiet," I once attempted to gently suggest to them. "Listen to you, you're a poet and you don't know it," she retorted. My cheeks stung with shame; if only it were true.

And so it went, for days. Trying to make the best of things, and be in the moment, I told myself repeatedly to forget my agenda. There was no rush to see the Atlantic Ocean, was there? Would it not be there whether I arrived now or later? We turned down this road, and that road, over hill, and over dale. We bought fresh peaches at a roadstand, and to this day, I have tasted none more delicious.

I had finally grown accustomed to the idea that it mattered little to have no idea where we actually were, when, noticing that cliché was finally asleep (and wind out of sight for the moment), I turned the radio knob away from the static we'd been listening to for the last few hours. I found an actual radio station playing

Miles Davis and it was like angel's breath. At last. Something to enjoy to myself, if only for a few brief but private moments.

"Oh, I love that song," cooed cliché sleepily, pushing the selector button back to static.

"I'd actually prefer the station I was listening to, thank you," I said, turning the knob back. At this, cliché bolted upright in her seat.

"You're a bore, daddy-oh," she said, pouting. "Word from the bird, you're a real wet rag. Are you going to let him talk to us like this, wind?"

I saw wind looking at me disapprovingly in the rear-view mirror.

"Yes, wind," I said through clenched teeth. "You seem content to let cliché speak for you all the time. I'm dying to hear what you think about all this. What's it gonna be? Music, static or nothing?!"

By way of an answer, wind blew open the back door and threw himself out of the car.

I slammed on the brakes, fishtailing to a stop several hundred feet down the road.

"Oh, my God, my God, oh my God," I stammered as I put on the emergency flashers. I steered over to the shoulder, put the car in park and jumped out.

I ran out into the road and down the yellow line, my eyes darting back and forth... but wind was nowhere to be found. No crumpled form, no bloody mess, nothing.

"wind? wiiiind?!" I called out. There was no reply. A manic search through the tall grass in the median yielded no sign of him, either.

"Can't find him, I bet?" I looked back to see a now kerchief and bikini-clad cliché sunbathing on top of the car. "Ha! Typical wind! What a banana!"

"What? You mean to tell me he's done this before?" I yelled back, incredulous.

"Oh, sure, Poindexter," she replied. "He's a very sensitive sort and he doesn't like confrontation. But he's got a stubborn streak a mile wide and when he doesn't get his way, there's no telling what he'll do or what he's capable of. But you had to have your music tuned to your station, so there you have it."

"Excuse me!?" I stammered, stomping back to the car with my fists clenched.

I was absolutely livid. "A maniac throws himself out of my car at sixty miles an hour and you're saying somehow it's my fault? That's insane! You're insane, forgive me for saying! Your friend might be lying dead in the ditch and you're sunbathing on the top of my car?! I mean, what the hell is wrong with you?!"

"Well, don't blow your jets, George, I'm

not making love to you if that's what you're
suggesting!" she snorted, jumping down from
the top of the car.

My face jammed in palsied confusion.
"What's wrong, chum, cat got your tongue?"
She grabbed my hand and pulled me towards
the woods. "You were making the king's jive
a moment ago and now I'm hep to your game
you're playing spazz?"

She deftly undid her bikini top with one
hand while unbuttoning my shirt with the other.
"Well, I'll hand it to you, Chauncey," she said,
using a judo hip-check to fling me to the ground.
"I didn't peg you for a bird dog, but you're fast."

She pulled off my pants and flung them
on the antlers of a deer as it ran by. "Well, see
here, I'm no kitten, but I am a lady!" Modesty
precludes further detail here, but my virginity
was thrown clear of the blast like an unwelcome
demon and ran gibbering into the woods,
overtaking the deer with my pants, never to be
heard from again.

<hr />

Later, after I'd changed into new clothes
from my duffle bag in the trunk and got back
into the car, cliché was now wearing pajamas,
and painting her nails. "He's crazy, wind! But we
can't wait here forever. He'll turn up when he's

good and ready and not a moment sooner."

I turned the key, put the car in gear and pulled back out onto the highway. "To be honest, I thought he'd never leave," she whispered conspiratorially. "Now I've got you all to myself."

Then, as the burnt orange-chocolate sunset sank behind us, she recited, from memory, what she claimed were passages from the Reader's Digest version of the *I Ching*. I just listened, amazed at the coincidence of how similar to fortune cookies they actually sounded.

And later after she'd fallen asleep on my shoulder, I pondered the state of my life to that moment. What had just happened? Why was I here? Why do you meet certain people at crucial moments in your life? What part of my journey was she here to help me with? What was she here to teach me?

"Ooh la la, c'est la vie," offered cliché drowsily as we passed the 'Bievenue' sign at the border into Quebec, and she changed the radio station without asking... again. I clenched my teeth... not only because the particular frequency she'd found was making my fillings hurt, but also because wind had returned; he was sitting on the hood of the car, batting at the antennae in the moonlight.

It was going to be a long ride to Halifax. And

that's why, at the back of my mind, a plan began
to hatch. I felt almost certain I could ditch them
in Montreal. But that, as they say – and as I do
now – is another story entirely.

Airport Cab

Grant Blant had just picked up his luggage from the carousel when he saw the man smiling at him from behind cheap sunglasses, under a tuft of unkempt brown hair that was greying at the temples.

"You lookin' for a cab?"

"Uh..." said Blant. "Yeah..."

He was indeed looking for a cab, but as friendly as this man was, Grant seemed to remember he'd heard somewhere that you should never to accept a ride from a cabbie inside the terminal.

"Where you headed? I'll take you," said the man, beginning to walk away before Grant could actually answer the questions.

Grant felt a bit wary; it all seemed too easy and too suspicious, but he was tired and just wanted to get to his hotel. The man looked like a cabbie, and when Grant watched him head towards the automatic glass doors under a sign that read 'TAXI', it seemed legit.

Grant picked up speed to catch up to the briskly walking man. "I'm over this way," said the cabbie, and Grant followed him along the line of parked taxis waiting for fares. But when they passed cab after cab parked in line, turned the corner and began walking to the end of the parking lot, Grant grew apprehensive.

"Are you supposed to grab customers right out of the terminal?" he asked.

"Listen, if I lived by the rules around here I'd never make a living," replied the man, leading him to a green dumpster with the word "CAB" written on it in spray paint. As he watched the man climb the rungs on it to lift the lid, Grant felt he had to protest.

"Okay, whoa," said Grant. "What is this?"

"This your first trip to New York, ain't it?" said the guy, with a touch of irritation.

"Forget this," said Grant, walking away, slowly at first, then breaking into a run back to the safety of the terminal. "Thanks for wasting my time, asshole!" the man yelled after him.

"Do we feed?" rasped a voice from inside the dumpster.

"Not yet, my master" said the man, with a bit of trepidation. "I'm sorry."

"Boo," growled the voice impatiently. "Methinks eating you instead."

"But then who would sing you to sleep, oh fiendish one?" stammered the man.

"Touche," said the dumpster voice.

Visions in White

The world had suddenly turned white; and Overlap Shorn now had no clue where he was going.

He'd been snowshoeing right behind his girlfriend, Joen. They'd seen the cottage at the far end of the open field, just a few kilometres away. But the wind had suddenly risen, kicking up clouds of snow, and now – Russell was alone as he could be, and no clue which direction was which.

"Joen!" he called. "Joen?!"

There was no answer but the blowing snow.

For months now, Overlap had felt their relationship was growing increasingly distant and strained. The things about her that he'd first loved were now slowly driving him crazy, and he imagined she probably was feeling the same way. Whereas in the beginning she had seemed interested in his work and the details of his day, hover the last few months he'd felt her grow distant and disinterested. Where once he'd thought of her as independent, she now seemed detached and aloof.

"Joen!" he called out again. "Joen?!"

Part of him was worried about how she was dealing with this sudden storm, but as he listened closely, and could hear nobody calling his name back, he realized the feeling in the pit of his stomach wasn't concern or panic at all.

It was resentment.

He was standing here, like an idiot, calling out her name, and she'd simply gone on without him. Why wasn't she looking for him? Why wasn't she calling for him?

Maybe that was it.

Maybe she really didn't care.

He couldn't see more than a foot away in any direction, with or without his protective visor. He felt abandonment, anger and panic jockey for position in his mind... and then... for some reason, he remembered something about the wise man knowing when the right thing to do is absolutely nothing.

So he stopped moving and just stood. And he took a deep breath in.

And out.

And he closed his eyes.

And he waited.

That's when the steam locomotive blew its horn, scaring him out of his skin as it bombed towards him, missing him by inches.

The wind shear nearly blasted him off his feet as it dopplered past, receding swiftly behind swirling curtains of snow. He could have sworn every window was open, full of leering timberwolves wearing parkas, all leaning out and licking their lips, glaring at him with fiery eyes.

The word 'hallucination' flitted about the periphery of his rational mind, failing to gain the attention of the rest of his mind, which at that moment was too engrossed in reacting to the call of the humpback whale that filled his ears.

He looked up and there it was, swimming lazily in the air above him, the echo of its song muted by curtains of snow, but no less melancholy or lonesome as it faded in the distance.

Then all was quiet.

And then he understood.

It seemed a ludicrous and unlikely metaphor, but he'd never had a vision before, so who was he to judge?

Joen was the steam train full of timberwolves and and he was a lovesick whale. She was going places, and he still had some wandering to do. He knew the relationship was over, and he felt sad, but underneath that, he felt something else.

He saw himself taking responsibility for his own happiness. He knew that before he could learn to love anybody and be happy in any relationship, he'd have to learn to love himself, first. He began to weep, and he fell first to his knees, then to his face.

Lights flashed before his eyes as consciousness left him.

And then he saw nothing.

Snow began to cover him, but within moments, a hundred white stoats scurried out of the storm and dug under him, hoisting him up on their tiny backs. Then, wailing and snarling like a convoy of tiny ambulances, they rushed him the remaining half-mile to the cabin.

As they ferried him up the front steps, Joen opened the door and bid them put him by the fire. Then they they disappeared, still wailing and wraithlike, back outside into the wind.

Then she sat by him, disappointed, and waited for him to regain consciousness.

She'd really hoped he was the one. But he wasn't, she realized, and she made a mental note to stop dating her patients, no matter how cute.

Speaking in Tongues

While on his lunch break, Brent decided to buy a new pair of shoes.

On the scale of shoe fussiness, he rated average, so after about 10 minutes he'd picked a style and tried them on. Then on impulse, he picked a more expensive pair he didn't really like as much, paid for those instead, and walked out of the store wearing them.

He was no sooner out on the sidewalk that he noticed his new shoes were squeaking.

Initially he thought it was not a big deal. He remembered his dad used to repeat one of those old French Canadian adages: "When your shoes squeak, it means you didn't pay for them." The funny part of that axiom, Brent realized, was that he had no proof that it was indeed old, French, or Canadian. It was also suspicious that his father had always spoken to him in Swedish.

"Well, Dad," thought Brent. "I definitely

paid for them. Just ask Visa."

But he noticed that as he got closer to his workplace, the squeaking was attracting a little unwanted attention.

The hot-dog vendor narrowed his eyes and watched him walk by disapprovingly.

A dog snarled and tried to nip him as he walked by.

An old Italian lady, draped in black mourning clothes for her twenty-years-dead husband, sneered and spat at him, giving him the evil eye.

A woman with a small child gasped at him and covered her child's ears. He couldn't figure out why a little shoe squeaking was garnering such negative attention.

He got back to his desk and sat down. His boss Joe leaned out of his office. "Brent," he said. "Can I see you in here for a second?"

"Sure thing," said Brent. As he got up and walked past his workmates, he heard his shoe squeak: "Fuck you, Linda, fuck you, Tyler, fuck you, Brian, fuck you, Helen, fuck you, Nancy..."

He stopped dead in his tracks when Linda, Tyler, Brian, Helen and Nancy's heads popped up over their open concept cubicles and they glared at him, narrow-eyed.

"New shoes," he said, lamely, and then walked a little more softly, to see if that would help.

"... fuck... fuck... fuck..." said the shoes, a little more softly than before.

He got to Joe's office and walked in. "Fuck you, Joe" said his shoes as he sat down. Joe stared at him.

"I'm so sorry," said Brent. "New shoes."

"You're fired," said Joe's cravat.

Mac Mollins Loved Snow

The neighbours all had snow blowers, but Mac Mollins was a traditionalist, and for his money, nothing could beat a shovel and a little hard work. And Mac seemed to have been blessed with a lot of hard work this winter.

His driveway had been filled with snow, storm after storm, and it had made him a happy man.

He'd often start shoveling hours before it had even stopped snowing, just doing his part to "keep winter green,' as he joked to the neighbours, most of whom didn't understand the mixed metaphor, and all of whom were weirded out by him.

Except for Yorl Yorlafsen.

To the neighbours, Yarl was just the local senior citizen pot dealer that everybody on the street visited once in a while. But this was just the form he'd assumed in this dimension, on

this little cul-de-sac in Moncton. In reality, Yorl
was a mystical Snow Praetor, who kept winter on
its proper schedule in this territory.

Yorl quite admired Mac's love of winter, often
watching from his window, pulling massive elk-
horn bong hits while bidding the snow sprites
to blow just the right amount of extra snow on
Mac's driveway, just to test him, to see if Mac
Mollins was indeed, as had been rumoured, a
being to whom a special gift might be bestowed.

Only once in every third generation, a truly
special human being, pure of heart and strong
of will, could be given a magical gift. If their
love of winter snow be pure, if their shoveling
were straight, virtuous and true, they would
be summoned to the great Winter Hall in
Blaetherland, where the White Council would
gift them with Snow Praetorhood. They would
gain eternal life and be granted a dominion of
their own to reign over, every winter, till the end
of days.

There was also an extremely generous points
club card.

And Mac was just one such mortal who
had gained the attention of the White Council
over these last few years. They had bade Yorl
keep a close eye on him, and for the last several
months, Mac had been so happily engrossed in

his shoveling that he'd failed to notice that it only ever snowed on his driveway – every day – even when it wasn't snowing anywhere else on the street.

But it now was late March, and spring was just around the corner; Mother Nature as always would have the final word, and she would be clear and firm on when Snow Praetors had had their fun and outworn their welcome for the season. Yorl felt it was time to reveal himself.

Tonight, Yorl decided he would let Mac in on the joke before he packed it in and went to his Antarctic timeshare for the summer. And if Mac took the news well, the next logical step would be to invite him to Blaetherland for the induction.

"Mac," said Yorl, appearing in a puff of smoke at the end of Mac's drive, just as the younger man had finished heaving the last shovelful of white stuff over the snowbank. (He could have walked, but since he was granting an invitation to Praetorhood, he figured he'd amp up the production value a tad.)

"Yorl," said Mac. "Nice to see you. Just got done shoveling here, perfect timing," he laughed.

Yorl chuckled. "Yeah, I like to make snow, not get rid of it so much."

"That's weird," said Mac.

"Is it?" chuckled Yorl.

"Yeah. Backasswards if you ask me," replied Mac, a little put off whenever he felt someone might be making fun of his ardor for shoveling.

"Well, I wanted to let you in on a little secret," said Yorl, and in the traditional (if somewhat overdone way of the Snow Praetors) he drew a huge hit of Norwegian Blue kush from his bong, and blew a cloud of mystic smoke into Mac's face.

Mac fell into a stupor instantly.

As the images of the winter-long gag played out to Mac's subconscious, his face flickered with emotions. He felt the victory of every time he'd cleared the driveway, and the anticipation of every early snowfall. He came to understand that it was Yorl who had made all this wonderful snow. He saw the neighbours laughing at him, but saw how proud Yarl had grown of him. And then, when he realized now that this wonderful winter was over, and that Yarl would be going away for the summer, his shoulders sagged in disappointment.

"No hard feelings?" said Yorl, extending his hand.

"No," lied Mac, still a little stunned. "No hard feelings..."

"Oh, and one more thing..." winked Yorl. "I have an offer to make if you ~" And there he stopped in mid-sentence, for that was when Mac swung the shovel hard, knocking Yorl out cold.

Mac looked up and down the street to be sure none of the neighbours were watching. Then, he dragged Yarl by his feet and tied him up in the shed.

"Looks like I got myself a snow maker," he giggled to himself, relishing the thought of how good shoveling in July was going to feel.

A Bee! A Bee!

It was a warm and humid summer's day in the late 1980s on a back road in rural New Brunswick.

A gentle breeze caressed the trees, rippling their leaves, exposing first their paler undersides and then their darker tops; nature's beautifully simple and ephemeral semaphore code.

The air was alive with insect song and the chirping of songbirds.

A bee, having spent the last ten minutes in a particularly aromatic and rich patch of clover, had just launched itself towards the roadside, rotating lazily to one side as it compensated for the extra weight of the cargo of pollen on its hind legs.

Down the road, a burgundy Toyota Tercel came around the corner.

Inside the car were four serious men.

A tall man.

A smoking man.

A short, fussy man.

A distracted man.

Inside the car were four serious men with a trunk full of shovels and tarps.

Inside the car were four serious men with a map to a box buried in a secret location in these back roads.

Inside the car were four serious men all plotting against each other as they listened to REM blasting from the tape deck.

Four men.

Tape deck.

Shovels.

Car.

Country road.

Summer breeze.

Open window.

A bee.

"Ahhh!" screamed the shotgun-riding, smoking man in falsetto notes that belied the stocky features of the bearded face from whence they emerged. "A bee! A bee!"

"Pull over!" yelled the back-seat men.

"A bee! A bee!"

The tall man slammed on the breaks and ran out of the car, as did the two back-seat men. But there was no escape for the bearded man. He was held back tightly in his seat by the protective hug of the seat belt, awakened from its slumber by the sharp brake slam, and intent on doing it's duty.

"Mragh! A bee! A bee!"

The bearded man was now a blur of flailing arms and legs, slapping and grasping and kicking in vain to release the belt clip.

"What bee?" yelled the driver. "I don't see a bee!"

"A bee! A fucking bee! It hit me right in the fucking face! Fwaugh!"

Then with a hard-won, resounding click, the bearded, smoking man was finally free from the seatbelt, and he ran from the car to the side of the road.

Four grown men.

Tercel with doors ajar.

A bee, cowering under the back seat.

Suspicion.

The four men eyed each other warily, keeping a safe distance from each other, each one standing at one corner of the car.

Four grown men.

Tercel with doors ajar.

Silence.

If viewed from the air in this time before drone photography, the writer of this tale might gratuitously describe what happened next using cardinal directions.

And so...

In an attempt to defuse the situation, the short, fussy man (who felt nobody ever listened to him in the first place) cleared his throat to speak.

Big mistake.

Startled by the sudden break in tension, the bearded man at the north-east corner of the car instinctively unleashed a spray of shuriken from the cigarette still hanging from his lip. Each star flew straight and true, burying themselves in the jugular of the short, fussy man at the south-east corner of the car.

In a protective reflex, the tall man at the north-west corner of the car then shot the bearded man to his left directly in the heart with a single nib from his mechanical pencil-gun, and (with one single lead left in the chamber) swiveled towards the nervous man at the south-west corner.

By this point, the short, fussy (and now dead) man with all the shuriken in his face had hit the ground. The force of the impact fired the gun strapped to his ankle. The bullet ricocheted first off the road, then off a tree, and then off a mailbox before burying itself in the skull of the tall man, who now toppled to the ground, also dead.

The distracted man was truly perplexed, as usual.

Although he'd been very clearly and properly briefed on his part in this mission, he'd really not been paying much attention. He began dancing around in a bewildered and meandering semi-circle at the side of the road, looking every which way to see if anybody, anywhere had seen what had just happened and could tell him what to do. Finally, unable to make heads or tails of any of it, he simply detonated the home-made explosive belt he was wearing.

Explosion.

Silence.

Bits of a distracted man raining back to the ground.

A country road.

A burgundy Tercel with doors ajar.

Four formerly serious, now completely dead men.

Remember the bee?

As it peered at the scene from the top of the back seat, its mandibles dropped open in disbelief. Were it possible for its eyes to widen to display the same state of mind, they would have done so, too.

Four dead men.

A Tercel with doors ajar.

Treasure map on the passenger seat.

Keys in the ignition.

A bee that knew how to drive stick.

The bee drove to the location of the treasure, albeit in the wrong gear. By the time it reached the location, the transmission flywheel was in pieces, but it didn't care; this car wasn't his.

But the treasure?

Yes, that was his now.

A bee?

A bee.

Acknowledgements

Thanks to you, the reader, for somehow ending up on this page. You are exactly where you need to be, in this book, and in life in general. You are great! Have a Fresca!

Thanks to Duncan McKenzie and MKZ Press for saying yes to cliché and wind go hitchhiking.

Thanks to mom and dad for that first time they read one of my stories and laughed out loud, and to my dad for assuring me that I could build things with pen, paper and ideas that he admired every bit as much as what I saw him building out of hammer, wood and nails.

Thanks to Mr. Zinck for grade 9 language arts, and that 'A' you gave me for the short story assignment on metaphors and similes. It was, like, the best!

Thanks to Kevin, my brother, who I would totally like to remind, again, that I forgive him entirely for the trampoline/popcorn incident. There's no point bringing it up again here, it was my own damn fault and in retrospect, going to the AC/DC concert on painkillers was totally worth it. Still, you might have offered to carry me on your shoulders out of there. Despite its name, one does not just magically *glide* up and out of Magnetic Hill, whether you're on crutches or not. Anyway, not a big deal. Shouldn't have brought it up. Moving on.

Thanks to *The Coincidence Men* for the constant challenges, the constant growth, and the constant laughs.

Thanks to the *Calithumpians* for my first writing and theatre gig, and the late and wonderful Diane London Pacey, for repeatedly telling me (and *Calithumpians* after me) to "write that down, Marcel!"

Thanks to Claude, Dan, Don, and Pierre. Thanks to Barry, Dana, Shawn, Bill, Tim and Kevin.

Thanks to everyone who provided blurbs, forewords and advance critiques in the front section of this book. You are insanely talented people and I am eternally grateful you took the time to read my work and say something nice. You are the best people. Thanks to Ali Eisner and Mike Butler.

And, best for last, thanks to Leah and Bella. I love you.

About the Author

A New Brunswicker of Acadian extract, Marcel St. Pierre is a writer, producer, comedian and improvisor who now calls Toronto home. He is a co-founder and former Artistic Director of *The Bad Dog Theatre Company* and has performed across North America as a member of comedy troupes like *The Stand-Ins, Monkey Toast, The Second City National Touring Company* and now with *The Coincidence Men.*

Marcel is a Promax/BDA Award-winner for his work as an on-air promo writer and producer, and was part of the Canadian Screen Award-winning team that produced CBC Television's *The Morgan Waters Show.* (Gemini for Best Youth Program, 2007) His writing has appeared on CBC, YTV, HGTV, *Food Network, The Comedy Network, Treehouse TV* and more.

cliché and wind go hitchhiking is his second book of humorous short fiction, preceded by *Vengeful*

Hank & Other Shortweird Stories, also published by MKZ Press.

Visit his website *www.shortweird.com* where you can listen to his *Shortweird Radio* sketch comedy albums, and follow him on Twitter, Facebook and Instagram *@shortweird*

Photo by: Ali Eisner

Made in the USA
Columbia, SC
13 March 2018